THE CONVERSATION CLUB

story and pictures by
Diane Stanley

SCHOLASTIC INC.

New York Toronto London Auckland Sydney

Copyright © 1983 by Diane Stanley Vennema.
All rights reserved. Published by Scholastic Inc., 555 Broadway,
New York, NY 10012, by arrangement with
Macmillan Publishing Company.
Printed in the U.S.A.
ISBN 0-590-20272-3

1 2 3 4 5 6 7 8 9 10   14   02 01 00 99 98 97 96 95

For my mother,
FAY SHULMAN,
who can join my club anytime

1. THE VISITOR

Peter Fieldmouse put away the last of his belongings in their proper places in his new house. He put the kettle on the fire to boil and sat down to listen. He wanted to learn what his new home sounded like. He wanted to smell the new smells and notice all the little things that made this place different from other places he had lived.

Peter heard the sound of dry leaves turning over in the wind.

He heard the burble of running water.

He heard a bird singing.

He heard the crunch of someone walking on dry leaves.

There was a knock on the door.

"I'm coming," called Peter as he jumped to his feet and hurried to the door.

"Welcome to this neck of the woods," said his visitor in a loud voice. "I'm Charlie."

Charlie leaned his face very close to Peter's and smiled very wide.

"I'm Peter," said Peter. "It is so very nice—"

"Isn't it?" beamed Charlie. He picked something up from the ground and carried it into Peter's house.

"Now," he said, "let's move on to the gift-welcome basket. Actually, the *basket* isn't a gift. It's mine, but the stuff inside is for you—little tokens from the local merchants, you know. For example, we have here a glow-in-the-dark yardstick that says, 'No One Can Measure Up To Handy Hardy.' That's from Handy Hardy's Hardware, of course. Here is a small box of instant mashed potatoes from Grocery-in-the-Oak, and a house plant from Kate's Green Thumb."

Charlie looked at the plant and quickly handed it to Peter. "Unfortunately, it seems to have died on the way."

There was a pause, then Charlie smiled brightly. "Now, last," he said, "but definitely not least, is this attractive magnetic bottle opener from the Open-All-Day-and-All-Night Convenience Store."

"Well, thank you very much," said Peter. His arms were full of free gifts, so he couldn't shake hands. "It was nice to meet you, Charlie."

"Hold it, hold it!" said Charlie. "There's more!"

"More gifts?" asked Peter, looking down at the heap in his arms.

"No, that's all you get," Charlie said briskly. "But I want to invite you to join our club. I know you'll fit right in."

"Club?" asked Peter. He had never belonged to a club before. It might be fun, but he wasn't so sure he would fit right in.

"It's the Conversation Club. We meet every Thursday afternoon. Oh, we are a great group, let me tell you."

Charlie began to wave his arms enthusiastically. "Now, Sam, he knows everything about cooking— French cooking, Chinese cooking, you name it. Fay is our space expert. The planets, the stars, she'll tell you all about them. Pearl tells ghost stories, *and* she makes them up herself."

Charlie turned and looked out the open door. "I'm the gardening expert. For example, I could tell you now that you ought to be getting your spring bulbs planted right away. The mole who owned this house before you didn't know beans about gardening, I can tell.

"Anyway, where was I? Oh, yes, the club. Nancy speaks on sports. She changes with the seasons, too. Right now she's doing football, and in the spring it's baseball, and so on. What's your subject?"

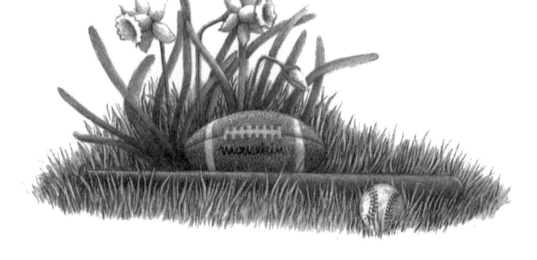

Peter looked at his shoes. There was a moment of silence.

"I don't think I have a subject," he said at last.

"Nonsense! Of course you do!" shouted Charlie.

"Excuse me, the water is boiling for my tea," said Peter, backing apologetically toward his kitchen.

"You can't do cooking," said Charlie, following him further inside. "I told you, Sam already does that."

Peter took two cups from the shelf and, after adding tea to the boiling water, poured it carefully through a strainer into the cups.

"Couldn't I just listen?" suggested Peter.

Charlie seemed to be turning this idea over in his mind. A gust of wind threw brown leaves up against the window.

"Stupendous idea!" said Charlie at last. "You can be the expert on listening. Oh, I really like that. Very original!"

"Thank you," said Peter shyly.

"So that's settled. The next meeting is Thursday at my house. Just ask anyone how to get there. Well, now I'm off. Things to do; places to go." Charlie picked up his basket and left without tasting his tea.

2. THE CONVERSATION CLUB

Peter was the last to arrive. As he removed his coat and muffler he saw that everyone was busy, bustling around and getting ready for the meeting to start. Someone—it had to be Fay—was taping a chart of the planets to the wall. Peter wondered what would happen to the wallpaper when she took it down.

"Hi, Peter," Charlie called. "Hey, everybody, this is Peter, our listening expert."

"Welcome, welcome," said another club member in a blue football jersey.

"You must be Nancy," said Peter.

"See," yelled Charlie, "didn't I say he was a listening expert?"

"And you're Pearl?" asked Peter, showing off a little. She nodded her head, which was covered by a large white veil.

Everyone returned to their busy preparations. They all had something to do except Peter. He felt small and left out.

At last Charlie tapped on the table. "Are we ready?" he asked.

They all nodded yes.

"Then let us begin."

The conversation began very softly, like a low buzzing. As it grew louder and louder, Peter could scarcely believe his ears. Everyone in the room was talking at once!

It sounded something like this:

"In the opening game you add some parsley stir the crocuses which resemble the sound of shrieking in our solar system for a first down mix in the garlic daffodils that faint at the sight of blood on Mercury or Venus bay leaf ran into the end zone, but roses are more fragrant and can fly to the haunted house of Jupiter with its quarterback seasoned with salt and pepper to taste."

When he could stand it no longer, Peter ran to the door, opened it, and bolted into the cold, clear, quiet afternoon.

Behind him, the room quite suddenly grew still, and then everyone rushed out of Charlie's house, astonished.

"Where are you going? What's wrong?" they all cried. "Come back!"

"I can't," said Peter, stopping. "It gives me a headache. You all talk at the same time!"

"But we all have such interesting things to say," Nancy said.

Peter looked at them all, took a deep breath and said, "Yes, I'm sure that you do. But I can't be in your club because I have a club of my own."

"What kind of club? Who's in it? Can I join?" they all asked together.

"It's a listening club; no one talks, and I am the only member."

Peter began to walk home. He wrapped his muffler around his neck.

"Wait! Oh, wait! Can't we join? Oh, please, next week can we come to your house? I can't wait. How exciting. Another club!" they all said at once.

"Well, I guess so. But you have to obey the rules. No talking." And he disappeared down the path.

Pearl watched him go. "You know what?" she said to the others. "Our conversation gives me a headache, too."

3. THE LISTENING CLUB

Snow had been falling all morning. The wind blew it against the few dry leaves still on the trees and made a rattling sound. In the quiet, Peter got the tea things ready. The room smelled of newly baked muffins. A fire crackled in the hearth.

They all came in together, along with a gust of cold air. They chattered excitedly as they hung up their coats and hats and mufflers. Peter wiped up the melting snow from the doorway and spread the towel under the coats to catch the drips. He poured tea and passed the steaming muffins as the club members found chairs and moved closer to the fire.

The room began to feel warm again. There were soft slurps and swallowing sounds. Charlie sighed, "Ummmmmm," and Pearl said, "Ahhhhh." Fay had brought her knitting. Her needles went *click-scratch, click-scratch*.

"Are we doing this right?" Sam asked at last.

"Oh, just great," Peter said.

The wind rattled the door. The bare branches of the tree scratched against the window. Charlie put his empty teacup on the floor.

Quietly he said, "You know, I can't help thinking about the bulbs I planted. I planted them in the
meadow instead of around the house. In the spring,
while there is still snow, there will be yellow and
purple crocuses. And later, when the grass is high,
there will be daffodils and tulips mixed together."

"Oh, how beautiful that will be," said Peter,
imagining it in his mind.

"Shhh!" said Nancy.

"Quiet!" said Sam.

Charlie leaned back in his chair, and looked out at the snowy meadow.

They all had more tea. The wind outside blew in heavy gusts against the house.

"Did you know," said Fay, "that the Great Red Spot on Jupiter is really a giant storm that blows in a circle? It is thirty thousand miles long and has been blowing for over three hundred years!"

"Wow!" said Peter. "Three hundred years!"

"Ahem," said Charlie.

"You're not being quiet," said Sam.

The wind began to howl in the chimney. The windows rattled. But it was warm around the fire. "My house is nicer with friends in it," thought Peter. *Screetch,* went the branch on the window pane, *rattle, rattle, rattle.*

"What a perfect setting for the ghost story I wrote last night," said Pearl.

"Well, you can't tell it," said Fay.

"I know, but I can't help thinking...."

"This is a listening club, not a thinking club," said Nancy.

"It's my club," said Peter, firmly. "And I just changed the rules. Let Pearl tell her story, and everyone else will listen. Just one at a time—that's the new rule."

So while the snow whirled outside the little house and the wind howled, the friends all listened while Pearl told her story.

It was the best they had ever heard.